A TANGRAM THEATR

THE RAGE OF NARCISSUS

BY SERGIO BLANCO
TRANSLATED & ADAPTED BY DANIEL GOLDMAN

The UK Premiere was first performed
at the Pleasance Theatre, Islington
Tuesday 18th February to Sunday 8th March 2020.

Pleasance Islington
Carpenters Mews
North Rd
London
N7 9EF
www.pleasance.co.uk

THE RAGE OF NARCISSUS
BY SERGIO BLANCO
TRANSLATED & ADAPTED BY DANIEL GOLDMAN

SAM CRANE | SERGIO BLANCO

Written by Sergio Blanco
Translated and Directed by Daniel Goldman

Designer Natalie Johnson
Lighting & Video Designer Richard Williamson
Sound Designer Kieran Lucas

Production Manager Sean Ford
Stage Manager Amy Spall

Casting Nadine Rennie CDG
Press Representative Kate Morely PR

Producers
Daniel Goldman for Tangram Theatre
Nic Connaughton for the Pleasance

CAST

SAM CRANE | SERGIO BLANCO

Sam Crane studied at Oxford University and trained at LAMDA.

His extensive theatre credits include …*Some Trace of Her, DNA, The Miracle* and *Sunset at the Villa Thalia* (National Theatre); *Othello, Henry IV (Part 1 & 2), All's Well That Ends Well, Bedlam, Eyam* (Shakespeare's Globe); *Ghosts* (Bristol Old Vic); *The Shawl* (Young Vic); *The Humans* (BAM New York). He was nominated for the Ian Charleson award for his performances in Ghosts and Othello.

Sam also played Winston Smith in Robert Icke's acclaimed production *1984* in the West End, and Farinelli in *Farinelli and the King* at The Globe, in the West End and on Broadway.

Sam's television credits include *Father Brown, New Tricks, Casualty, Poirot; Murder on the Orient Express, Doctors, Midsommer Murders* and *Sins*. He played one of the leads in *Desperate Romantics* and has guest starred in BBC's *Call the Midwife* and *Poldark, Fearless* and *Endeavour* for ITV, and in Series 2 of Netflix's *The Crown*.

Film work includes *The Christmas Candle* and *The Appointment*, directed by Alexandre Singh.

Sam's most recent credits include series roles in BBC One's *The Trail of Christine Keeler*; and will soon be seen in the eagerly anticipated series *Cobra* for Sky One..

CREATIVE TEAM

SERGIO BLANCO | *WRITER*

Sergio Blanco is a Franco-Uruguayan playwright and director. His work – which has been translated, published and performed throughout the world – has been awarded the National Playwriting Award of Uruguay, the Playwriting Award of the Municipality of Montevideo, the Prize of the National Fund Theatre, the Florencio Award for Best Playwright, the International Casa de las Americas Prize, an Off West End Award, and The Theatre Award for the Best Text in Greece.

His other works include: *'45, Slaughter, Opus Sextum, Kassandra, El Salto de Darwin, Tebas Land (Thebes Land), El Bramido de Düsseldorf,* and his most recent play *Cuando pases sobre mi tumba.*

DANIEL GOLDMAN | TRANSLATOR, ADAPTOR, DIRECTOR

Daniel trained in theatre at Escuela Andamio 90 (Buenos Aires) and École Jacques Lecoq (Paris).

Directing credits include: *Frankenstein* (Inside Out Theatre, Beijing), *Oedipus at Colonus* (Cambridge Arts Theatre), *Camasca* (Teatro Britanico, Lima), *Thebes Land* (Arcola), *James Rowland's Songs of Friendship* (Vault Festival, Edinburgh Fringe Fringe, UK / International Touring), *John Hinton's Scientrilogy* (Edinburgh Festival Fringe, UK / International Touring), *The Dragon* (Southwark Playhouse), *Waheri Wanawake Wa Windsor* (Shakespeare's Globe, National Theatre of Kenya, International Touring), *Fuente Ovejuna* (Southwark Playhouse), *You're not like the other girls Chrissy* (Edinburgh Festival Fringe, Bush Theatre / Co-directed with Omar Elerian), *Fucked* (Old Red Lion, Edinburgh

Festival Fringe) and *Richard III* (Southwark Playhouse / Co-directed with Donnacadh O'Briain).

Translation / adaptation credits include: *Frankenstein, Thebes Land, The Dragon, Waheri Wanawake Wa Windsor, Fuente Ovejuna.*

NIC CONNAUGHTON | PRODUCER

Nic is a Director, Dramaturg, Programmer and Producer. He is currently Head of Theatre for the Pleasance Theatre Trust, overseeing the organisation's theatre programme at their London base Pleasance Islington, and at Pleasance Edinburgh every August for the Edinburgh Festival Fringe. He was formerly Associate Producer at Arcola Theatre in Dalston, where he lead on New Work Development and Creative Engagement.

Producing credits at Pleasance Islington include: *Sink The Pink present Escape From Planet Trash* (2019); *In Lipstick* (with Up In Arms and Ellie Keel Productions, 2019); and *Sink The Pink present How To Catch A Krampus* (2018). As an Associate Producer at Pleasance Islington: *No Sweat* (with Reece McMahon Production, 2020); *The Fix* (with 2020); and *Ali and Dahlia* (Nominee, Writers' Guild of Great Britain - Best New Play 2019).

NATALIE JOHNSON | DESIGNER

Natalie trained at The Liverpool Institute for Performing Arts and was awarded the Liverpool Everyman and Playhouse Prize for Stage Design in 2017.

Design credits include: *The Shadow* (Home MCR), *Tick Tick Boom* (Bridge House Theatre) *Bluebeard* (Alphabetti Theatre), *Catching Comets* (The Pleasance, Royal Exchange Studio), *Twelfth Night* (Bridge House Theatre and Globe Neuss, Germany), *Mydidae* (Hope Mill Theatre), *Striking 12* (Union Theatre), *Putting It Together* (Hope Mill Theatre), *Eris* (The Bunker), *To Anyone Who Listens* (Hen and Chickens), *The Wasp* (Hope Mill Theatre), *Othello* (Everyman Theatre)

RICHARD WILLIAMSON | LIGHTING & VIDEO DESIGNER

Richard trained at LAMDA, is Head of Production for C venues at the Edinburgh Festival, and is a Trustee of the Kings Head Theatre.

Previous work includes: The Olivier award winning *Rotterdam* (West End/Off-Broadway/UK National Tour); *Richard III*, *An Arab Tragedy* (Swan Theatre Stratford/ International tour); *Sampled* and *Danse Élargie* (Sadler's Wells); *Great Expectations* (UK tour); *Little Miss Sunshine* (Arcola Theatre and UK Tour); *Fiddler on the Roof* and *The Comedy about a Bank Robbery* (Istanbul); *Beowulf, Septimus Bean and His Amazing Machine, Jason and the Argonauts* (Unicorn); What's On Stage 'Best Production' Winner *Thebes Land* (also video), *New Nigerians, Drones Baby Drones* (also video), *Shrapnel* (also video), *Mare Rider, Macbeth, A Midsummer Night's Dream, The Country* (Arcola Theatre); *A Political History of Smack and Crack* (Edinburgh Fringe and Soho Theatre); *Oedipus at Colonus* (Cambridge Arts Theatre); *The Body* (Barbican); *The Dark Side of Love* (Roundhouse); *In My Name, Boris World King* (Trafalgar Studios); *Thrill Me* (Tristan Bates/Charing Cross Theatre/UK and international tour); *Twentieth Century Boy* (New Wolsey Ispwich); and *Strangers In Between* (Trafalgar Studios and Kings Head)

KIERAN LUCAS | SOUND DESIGNER

Kieran is a sound designer and theatre-maker. He is a founding member of Barrel Organ theatre company & associate artist at Coney.

Sound & composition credits include: *Antigone* (New Diorama), *GASTRONOMIC* (Shoreditch Town Hall/ Norwich Theatre Royal), *Found Sound* (Coventry Cathedral), *CONSPIRACY* (Underbelly/New Diorama), *Pops* (HighTide Festival) *Companion: Moon* (Natural History Museum), *Mydidae* (Hope Mill), *How We Save The World* (Natural History Museum), *The Ex-Boyfriend Yard Sale* (CPT/Progress Festival), TBCTV (Somerset House), *Square Go* (Paines Plough Roundabout/59E59), *The Drill* (BAC/UK Tour), *A Girl In School Uniform (Walks Into A Bar)* (New Diorama) - Off-West End Award & Theatre and Technology Award nominated for Best Sound Design, *My Name Is Rachel Corrie* (Young Vic), *BIG GUNS* (The Yard), *Under The Skin* (St. Paul's Cathedral), *Some People Talk About Violence* (UK Tour).

SEAN FORD | PRODUCTION MANAGER

Sean studied at Oxford University before running away to the Circus and working in the International Festival Circuit.

Production Management credits include: Gecko's *The Wedding* (International Touring - Barbican), Gecko's *Missing* (International Touring - Battersea Arts Centre), *Superblackman* (Battersea Arts Centre), *The Market Project* (Pleasance Theatre), *The Incident Room* (New Diorama Theatre), *Potted Potter* (Australasia Tour 2020).

Sean is the Head of Production for the Pleasance at the Edinburgh Fringe Festival.

AMY SPALL | STAGE MANAGER

Amy is a London based Freelance Stage Manager having trained at Mountview Academy of Theatre Arts.

Stage Management Credits include: *A Monster Calls*, *Afterglow* (Southwark Playhouse), *Horrible Histories* (Apollo Theatre), *Polyeucte* (UCL), *Woman Before A Glass*, *Agnes Colander* and *Stitchers* (Jermyn Street Theatre), *Midlife Cowboy* (Pleasance Theatre).

NADINE RENNIE CDG | CASTING DIRECTOR

Nadine was in-house Casting Director at Soho Theatre for fifteen years; working on new plays by writers including Dennis Kelly, Bryony Lavery, Arinzé Kene, Roy Williams, Philip Ridley, Laura Wade and Vicky Jones.

Since going freelance in January 2019 Nadine's credits include *The Glass Menagerie* and *Hoard* (Arcola Theatre), *Good Dog* (Tiata Fahodzi), *Little Baby Jesus* (Orange Tree Theatre), *The Last King of Scotland* (Sheffield Crucible), *Random* and *There Are No Beginnings* (Leeds Playhouse), *The Little Prince* (Fuel Theatre), *Price* (National Theatre of Wales) and continues to cast for Soho Theatre - most recently *Run Sister Run* and *The Special Relationship*.

TV work includes: BAFTA-winning CBBC series *Dixi*, casting the first three series.

Nadine also has a long-running association as Casting Director for Synergy Theatre Project and is a member of the Casting Directors Guild.

PLEASANCE THEATRE TRUST

Pleasance Edinburgh opened as part of the 1985 Festival Fringe with two theatres facing onto a deserted courtyard-come-car-park at an unfashionable eastern end of Edinburgh's Old Town. Thirty seasons later the Pleasance has become one of the biggest and most highly respected venues at the Edinburgh Festival Fringe, with an international profile and a network of alumni that reads like a Who's Who of contemporary comedy, drama and entertainment.

Pleasance Islington has been one of the most exciting Off-West-End theatres in London since it opened its doors in 1995, providing a launch pad for some of the most memorable productions and renowned practitioners of the past decade and staying true to its mission of providing a platform for the talent of the future. Across three spaces, the theatre welcomes artists at all stages of their careers, with a commitment to new work that pushes boundaries.

Pleasance Islington plays host to some of the biggest names in comedy and the likes of Michael McIntyre, Russell Brand, Micky Flanagan, Mark Watson, Adam Hills and Mark Thomas have all regularly complimented our comedy programme.

TANGRAM THEATRE

Since being founded in 2006, Tangram has created a wide range of critically acclaimed new plays, reimagined classic texts and devised pieces, including *4.48 Psychosis* (ORL & Arcola), *Crunch!* (Edfringe, UK & Int. Touring), *Richard III* (Southwark Playhouse), *Fucked* (ORL & Edfringe), *John Hinton's Scientrilogy - The Origin of Species, Albert Einstein: Relativitively Speaking, The Element in the Room* (Edfringe, UK & Int. Touring), *Fuente Ovejuna* (Southwark Playhouse), *The Dragon* (Southwark Playhouse) and James Rowland's *Songs of Friendship Trilogy - Team Viking, A Hundred Different Words for Love, Revelations* (Vault Festival, Edfringe, UK & Int. Touring).

As a company, we aim to make theatre that is surprising, irreverent and life-affirming, where content determines form. As storytellers, we want to talk about the world we live in. As idealists, we believe that theatre can make the world a better place. As people, we want to make real connections with audiences and other artists. As a result, we're interested in work that breaks the fourth wall and actively engages our audiences.

What's in a name?

A tangram is an ancient Chinese puzzle comprised of seven geometrical shapes (five triangles, a parallelogram and a square) that can be put together to form a perfect square or be reconfigured to make an infinite number of new shapes. As Tangram Theatre Company, we approach every project as an opportunity to bring different people and ideas into the same space and explore the infinite possibilities that such a coming together invites.

THE RAGE OF NARCISSUS

Sergio Blanco

THE RAGE OF NARCISSUS

Translated and adapted by Daniel Goldman

OBERON BOOKS
LONDON

WWW.OBERONBOOKS.COM

First published in 2020 by Oberon Books Ltd
521 Caledonian Road, London N7 9RH
Tel: +44 (0) 20 7607 3637 / Fax: +44 (0) 20 7607 3629
e-mail: info@oberonbooks.com
www.oberonbooks.com

PB ISBN: 9781786828552
E ISBN: 9781786828545

Cover photography: Ali Wright
Cover design: Harry Neal

Printed and bound in the UK.

Visit www.oberonbooks.com to read more about all our books and to buy them. You will
also find features, author interviews and news of any author events, and you can sign up for
e-newsletters and be the first to hear about our new releases.

Printed on FSC® accredited paper

10 9 8 7 6 5 4 3 2 1

Characters

SERGIO BLANCO

SAM CRANE

Author's Note

The entire play takes place in room 228, City
River Hotel, Ljubljana, Slovenia. Or perhaps it
takes place in Tivoli Forest. Or perhaps it takes
place somewhere else.

The poet is a fraud
His forgery is so complete
He comes to pretend that he is pain
Pain that you should feel.

Fernando Pessoa
'Autopyschography'

PROLOGUE

Hello and good evening. I hope you are well. Thank you for being here. Really. Thank you.

Before we start, I'd like to make something clear, which is that I am not Sergio Blanco. My name is Sam. Sam Crane. In other words, who you're looking at is not Sergio Blanco. Or, perhaps a better way of putting it is that this person standing here in front of you is not Sergio Blanco but Sam Crane. Now, I will do everything in my power to be like Sergio. To be him. And even that's not right because I won't be trying to be Sergio, but a character version of Sergio, Sergio as character. Clear? Everyone good? In summary. I will make every effort possible to be him and I ask that you all make every effort possible to believe that I am him.

One morning last May I received a phone call from Sergio. He was calling from Ljubljana. It was the first time he spoke to me about this piece. It was a very short conversation. Before putting the phone down he told me he would send me an email with more details. Two hours later I switched on my computer and there was an email from Sergio. I opened it with excitement, the excitement I feel every time I open an email from Sergio. In the email, Sergio was asking me to be a part of this piece. It was impossible to say no. That is how all of this began.

I have the email here and I'd like to read it to you.

'My brother, as I just told you on the phone, I am in Ljubljana. I came here to give a talk on Narcissus at the University's Department of Philology. The city is beautiful and the men are amazing. Anyway, I'm writing to you because I'm writing a new play, inspired by this city. It's a fable. I am going to write it for you. Yes. Sam, I would like you to be in it. To interpret it. To do it. Everything bar perform it. I propose that we do it next year. Daniel will direct it. We'll open in London and then we'll tour it. Lots of theatres in London have been asking me for a new show since *Thebes Land*. Please say yes. If you say no, then I'll stop writing it right now, and then, my life, you will be responsible for its non-existence. A thousand kisses everywhere. I. Sergio.'

1.

All of this happened some time ago.

Sam started with a clarification and I would like to do the same and make a second thing clear before we start. This isn't a monologue. It isn't a one-man show. It isn't a soliloquy. It's a story. A tale if you will. And like all tales, it will edge forwards bit by bit towards its conclusion over the next hour and a half. And so I would like to ask you for your patience and that you give yourselves over to a progression that won't always be dramatic but rather very often narrative.

Good, now, we can start.

As I already mentioned to you, all of this happened some time ago. The Department of Philology of the University of Ljubljana had invited me, Sergio, to give a talk at an international symposium on the theme of Myth and the Gaze.

Gaze. As in G. A. Z. E. Not...

No sooner had I landed at Ljubljana airport, it was a Monday, it was midday, than they took me to the hotel where I would be staying for the week. The name of the hotel was the City River Hotel and my room was room number 228.

The room was this one. This exact room.

As soon as I entered the room, I felt something strange, but at the time, I didn't realise what it was.

Then I did what I always do when I arrive at a hotel where I am going to be staying for a while. I unpacked my suitcase. I prepared my desk. I plugged in my computer, put my iPhone on charge and I logged onto the wifi with the code they'd given me at reception.

Then I undressed, I had a shower, and I lay down on the bed and opened up a dating app to see if I could get anyone to come by who would want to have sex as much as I did.

There were a couple of men online and one in particular caught my interest. He was 35 and he was three hundred metres away from the hotel. I sent him a message.

Hey!

He replied.

Sex now?

Why not?

A few more questions followed and then we began to send each other photos. Front on. Face. Torso. From behind.

Boundaries?

None.

Drugs?

Why not?

Within five minutes, we had agreed to meet at the hotel. Here. It was the most convenient option for me.

2.

Half an hour later, there was a knock on the door.

He was much more attractive than in his photo. I let him in and right away we began to fuck. We undressed and fucked all afternoon. We finished and restarted a number of times.

It was my first time with a Slovenian. His name was Igor and he lived in the outskirts of Ljubljana. That's all he told me that first time. He spoke a few words of Spanish.

Afterwards, when we were showering together, he asked me what I did, and as always happens when anyone asks me that question, I didn't know how to reply.

Shall we see each other again? He asked me before he left.

Let's see, I replied. I'll be here all week.

I can stay a little longer, he proposed, as I was accompanying him to the door.

I'd rather you didn't, I said. It's already nine and tomorrow I've got to be up at six /

So early?

Yes. I go running.

Every morning?

Every morning. I need to go to bed now.

Then he left, I checked my emails, I took my anti-depressants and then I lay down in bed to watch a nature programme on National Geographic about the extinction of the Bengal Tiger and I fell asleep within minutes.

3.

For some reason, I woke suddenly around two in the morning and felt the same sensation of strangeness that I had had when I first entered the room. I turned on the light, looked at the clock, saw that it was 2:05 a.m. and that was when, all at once, I saw it.

It was a stain. A dark stain on the carpet. It was near the bed. There. Here. Right here. It was a blood stain.

I got out of bed and I went closer to have a better look.

It was a dried out blood stain. It had been there for a while.

Suddenly, I realised that just next to it was another stain. A little smaller but also a blood stain. And when I looked closer at that one, I noticed there was another one next to that one too. That's when I moved the bed across and I saw that there were many more blood stains under the bed. One big one in the centre surrounded by a galaxy of smaller satellites all around it. And they were all the same colour. A dark brownish red. At first I felt a little disgust, but little by little the feeling of disgust was replaced by a sort of uneasiness.

Where had those blood stains come from?

I rolled the bed back to its original place, put on some clothes and I went down to reception to ask them if they could please give me another room.

Is something wrong?, they asked me.

I didn't want to explain or go into details.

It's a very noisy room, I can hear everything that's happening in the street and I can't sleep, is what I told them.

They explained to me that there was nothing they could do right then. That the hotel was fully booked. But that they would try to move me the next day.

I asked them to please try.

Then I went back to my room, but I found it impossible to go back to sleep. I couldn't stop thinking about the stains.

Why were they there? What had happened?

Finally at three, I decided to take a sleeping pill and little by little I slipped into a deep sleep.

4.

The next morning, before going for my run, I went back to reception and reminded them of my request to change room. They told me that they would do everything they could but that they couldn't make any promises. The hotel was fully booked, in part because of the symposium in which I had come to participate.

At 6:10 I went out on a 45 minute run.

The city was completely empty at that time in the morning. I ran to Tivoli Park which was where reception had recommended I go, and once there, I began to follow one of the paths that went into the poplars.

It was the month of May. It was spring. In the far distance, you could see the Alps still covered in snow.

As I ran, I practiced my talk. I was trying to remember it. To order it. To time it right.

I had decided to speak about the gaze in the myth of Narcissus and the title that I had given my talk was 'The Poetic Gaze of Narcissus: The Transformation of Reality' … But I don't want to get ahead of myself. We're getting ahead of ourselves. We'll come back to this soon. I promise. Now, let us return to the tale.

5.

After running for 45 minutes I returned to the hotel and, after having had a very hot shower, I went down to have breakfast with some of my colleagues from other European universities, who had just arrived.

Everyone was saying the same thing, how pleasant the city was. And it was true. The city was a delight. And everyone was also commenting on how generous the Slovenians were. And then after that came the unavoidable comments on how beautiful the Slovenian language was. And after a few minutes everyone would surely move on to say how delicious the local food was.

In these sort of congresses, outside of the giving of the talks themselves, where each participant would unfurl with false modesty their latest findings in order to impress the rest of their colleagues, there were always these same banal exchanges, devoid of all interest. Everyone was very happy to talk about the beauty of Ljubljana's streets but no one could bring themselves to talk about the rise of the extreme right in the most recent elections that had taken place only a few days earlier. Little by little, political parties representing the neo-Nazis, racists, antisemites, Islamophobes and homophobes were gaining strength in parliaments across all of Europe. The ashes of Auschwitz were still warm and Europe was once again stoking the fire to light the flames. But no one had anything to say about such things. Not at these sorts of academic comings-together. No, at these sorts of academic comings-together, it was better not to speak about such things,

After breakfast, the majority of my colleagues had decided to visit the city. I chose to stay in the hotel to go over my emails and make some corrections to my conference. Also, I didn't like to visit cities with anyone else. The only person I liked to do so with was my mother. Nobody else.

6.

When they all left, I went up to my room and as soon as I was inside, I could see the blood stains. They were even more disturbing by day. The morning light brought them out. They were redder.

Slowly, I moved one of my hands towards one of the stains, and I did what I had been unable to do the night before, I touched it. Like this. As though I needed to check that the stains weren't wet. That they were dry.

It was evident that someone had tried to clean them but that they'd not been able to get the stains out.

All of a sudden, I realised that there were more blood stains on one of the walls. The colour was a little different, a little paler, but they were the same kind of stains and someone had tried and failed to make them disappear as well.

I tried to work a bit but I was having difficulties concentrating.

After a while, I decided to go for a walk. I needed to get out of my head. Clear my mind. Brighten my thoughts. Some fresh air would do me good.

So I decided to go to the Museum of Natural History. It was the only museum in the city that I was interested in visiting. From what I'd read, it housed a mammoth skeleton that was the oldest found in Europe.

7.

The museum was incredible. And best of all, it was completely empty. In recent years, people had stopped visiting such museums. It's understandable. In today's day and age there is nothing more obsolete than a museum of natural history. Why leave the house to visit glassed off exhibits of fossils, stuffed birds and amphibian skeletons, when you can go online in the comfort of your own home and see incredible animations that bring these fossils and birds and amphibians back to life. Perhaps, in a few years, these kinds of museum will disappear. Natural history museums will become fossils of themselves.

After putting in my earphones and selecting Bach's Cello Suites, I began to slowly make my way through the rooms.

I walked through huge rooms filled with reptiles, embalmed fish, massive tortoise shells, thousands of butterflies in dusty cabinets and hundreds more skeletons of apes, whales and pelicans.

And so, on and on I went, until I finally arrived at the room with the famous mammoth skeleton.

He was immense. Exquisite. A structure of hundreds of graceful bones that rose together in the centre of the room as though a prehistoric cathedral. He was the oldest example found on the continent. I went closer and, without anyone seeing me, I gathered my courage and I brought my hands to him and I began to caress him. I let my hands gently trace every bone. The femurs. The tibias. The ribs. I suddenly felt something in my throat. And then in my chest. Here. Right here. As though for a few seconds something stopped inside me, while I understood somewhere deep down that I was touching something very distant and alien, and at the same time very close and known.

Then I sensed that someone was coming and I took my hand away and without taking my eyes off him, I stood there for some minutes in silence.

8.

When I left the museum, I realised I was hungry and, rather than go through the tiresome process of choosing a restaurant and pointing at a menu and asking questions in a language I didn't speak to a waiter who also didn't speak it, about a cuisine that I knew nothing about, I went to the McDonald's across the street and I got myself a cheeseburger, medium fries and a Coke.

Having eaten with great discipline every last crumb and rooted out every last fry from the bottom of the bag, I walked back to the hotel. I wanted to do a bit of work on my talk, especially the beginning. I thought it would be best to start by thanking the interpreters who would be simultaneously translating my Spanish into more than twenty languages.

Not only thank them but also ask for their forgiveness. With me, they wouldn't be encountering the elegant Castilian of the Iberian peninsula, but rather a Spanish that was dry, raw and crude. No. Not crude. Crude is a horrible term. Coarse. Coarse is better. Or muddy. A Spanish that was as muddy as the waters of the Rio de la Plata that bathes the banks of Montevideo, which is the city where I was born. No, not where I was born. The city where I come from. And on top of that, they'd be translating the words of someone who doesn't even like, who despises, who doesn't even like his own language and who has exiled himself from his country to live in another, and whose Spanish is error-ridden, broken, wounded... a language in which he, in which I am only able to understand myself when I write it, but when I speak it, I...

So I opened my computer to begin to rewrite the beginning, and it was at that precise moment that I was interrupted by a call.

It was Igor.

He wanted to know if we could see each other again. I told him I was busy. That I would I would call him when I'd finished my work. He asked me several times when that would be. I told him it wouldn't be before Friday.

So you didn't like me.

No. That's not it. I liked you very much. But I'm working.

You'll only be here one week. Why don't we take advantage of that? I could come to the hotel at any time?

I had to tell him several times no. And that besides, I would prefer it if we didn't see each other at the hotel. That it was filling up with colleagues. That I would prefer to meet somewhere else.

Did you go to run this morning?, he asked me.

Yes.

Where?

To Tivoli. To the park.

Did you sweat?

Of course. A lot.

It must be a turn-on to see you running all wet with sweat.

Sorry, are you getting turned on?

It seemed to me that Igor was getting turned on at the other end of the phone line and so was I.

Yes. Yes. I'm hard.

Me too.

That's what I'm hoping. If you like, we can wank each other off.

OK. But nothing else. I have lots of work. Just a wank.

And that's what we did.

After hanging up, I had a shower, dressed and I went to the inauguration of the symposium.

9.

At the inauguration, we all continued in our hypocritical vein of always. We introduced each other to colleagues, we handed over business cards and we pretended to show interest in the person in front of us, even though, in reality, all we wanted to do was retire as early as possible to our hotel rooms to watch Netflix or, in my case, a National Geographic nature documentary.

Here too we exchanged the same banalities as always. We spoke in great detail about the canapés and the temperature of the champagne.

We did not speak about the fact that 65 Libyans had drowned when their boat capsized off the coast of Tunisia only the week before. If anyone had tried to bring that up, everyone would have looked at the floor or at the ceiling while trying to find a way of changing the subject.

This was the intellectual milieu of the top European universities. This was the legacy of Erasmus and Dante: that we popped into our mouths confit dates with Roquefort while the Mediterranean sea became an immense watery graveyard for migrants and refugees.

10.

When I got back to the hotel, on opening the door to my room, the first thing I did was to go straight over to the stains. Now, it was the first thing I did every time I entered my room. As if I needed to know that the stains were still there. That I hadn't invented it all in my head.

As I stooped down to look at them, I felt a strong desire for sugar. So I went to the minibar and took out an ice cold Coca Cola. This was a habit that I'd picked up from my time in the clinic. The doctors would always insist that every time we needed sugar, that we shouldn't repress that desire, especially in times of abstinence.

And it was just then, as I opened the can, that I saw that my mum was calling me on Skype.

I was tired and I wanted to go to sleep, but even so, I picked up. I'd come to an agreement with my sisters that I would talk to her every couple of days.

Hello Mum. Can you see me? I can see you. Can you hear me? OK. Hang on. How about now? I can hear you. Can you hear me? Are you by yourself? OK, good. How are you? What? No. It's me, Mum. I'm in Ljubljana. Do you remember that I told you I was going to Ljubljana? Ljubljana, Mum. In Slovenia. Yes. Yes, it's a real place. Yes, it's real. It's near Venice. Venice. What? No. No. I didn't call you. You called me. I'm in a hotel. I am in a hotel. This is a hotel room. A hotel, Mum. No. No. It's me, Mum. Look at me. Here. Mum. Hello. Mum. Did you hang up? Mum.

For the past few months, all conversations with my mother had become circular and twisting. Most of my efforts were concentrated on trying to make her understand who I was. Alzheimers had discombobulated her brain just like a powerful new computer virus hacking into an unprotected software programme. The doctors had told us it was only going to get worse.

At first, this way of communicating had been very distressing, then it became ridiculous, and finally a real waste of time that exhausted me.

My mother had become a sorry pixelated shadow of the person she had once been, the idea being to get her into a nursing home as soon as possible so that we, my sisters and I, could free ourselves from the weight that she had become.

After our Skype ended, I undressed, took an anti-depressant and went to bed.

I thought I'd have another wank. I started but I couldn't concentrate. The image of my mother and her galloping Alzheimers kept intercepting the images of naked hard-cocked men I was trying to focus on in order to become hard myself. After a few failed attempts, I made one final effort to exorcise the image of my mother's face from my mind's eye, and finally I managed to expel her and focus, but little by little I felt myself losing strength. I was tired. Very tired.

I ended up gently stroking myself, and within a few minutes, I fell asleep, holding my limp member, dead to the world, in my hand.

11.

It must have been 2:00 a.m. when I woke up again. Again at 2:00 a.m.. I felt awful. I was covered in sweat. I'd had a terrifying nightmare. I couldn't remember it at all, only that it had been terrifying.

I brushed the covers away and sat up on the edge of the bed.

I felt the same desire I'd had earlier for some sugar and it was then, as I was crossing the room to get another Coke from the minibar, that I noticed the blood stains again. But now they looked different.

Menacing.

The moonlight had changed their aspect.

I got closer to them and felt a need to touch them. To stroke them.

What had happened in this room? To whom had this blood belonged?

And slowly, without my noticing it was happening, I fell asleep on the carpet. Like this. Exactly like that. In that very position, I fell asleep.

12.

The next morning, when I woke up, I realised I'd fallen asleep on one of the stains. When I opened my eyes, it was the first thing I saw. It was early. Six in the morning. My whole body was tense. Especially around my neck. Just here. Before I went out for my run, I thought it best to have a steaming hot shower to try to relax my back muscles a little.

Afterwards I took my vitamins, put on my Nikes and I started out on my 45 minute run.

I had decided that as I ran, I'd go over the first part of my lecture. I'd divided it into three parts.

The first part was very important, because it was where I established my first reason for my theory that Narcissus's gaze was a metaphor for the artist's gaze. And the first reason was this. I believe that Narcissus's gaze is a gaze that is self-reflective, while searching for the other. In this way, the gaze of Narcissus is a gaze that invites the blurring of the self and the other. That's to say that we're dealing with a gaze that encounters itself and, at the same time, in that very instant of self-contemplation of the id, proposes an interrogation of the other. According to Pausanias, Narcissus, on seeing himself, sees the face of his dead twin sister. He sees himself and he sees the other. And this refractory mechanism by which I search for myself and find the other is similar to the artistic process that is in a constant fluctuation and oscillation between the self and the other. For example, in my own work, in my own writing, I am always present myself. I always start a story from personal experience, something I have lived, something that reflects my own experience, and, just like Narcissus, I always do this with the desire to go further, to exist outside of my own self, to be able to look at and find the other. Perhaps Rimbaud said it best when he said: *Je est un autre.*

I is an other.

Suddenly, as I was repeating this phrase of Rimbaud's in my head, I got the impression that someone was following me. I turned around and there he was.

It was him. It was Igor. He'd been running behind me. He was covered in sweat.

What are you doing?

I wanted to see you.

You scared me.

I didn't mean to.

Have you been following me for a while?

Yes.

And why didn't you say something?

I wanted to run after you. I like watching you from behind.

His body, covered in a film of sweat, and his wet hair were so much more arousing than when we'd first slept together in the hotel room. I had this sudden urge to touch him. Kiss him. Caress him. Right then.

Are you hard?

A little.

Me too.

And so we went off into the poplars and we began to fuck.

Just there.

Here.

As soon as we finished, we went our separate ways, he one way, I the other.

13.

When I made it back to the hotel, I bumped into some of my colleagues who were coming down to breakfast.

You look like you've been to the war and back, said one.

I was running in Tivoli Park and because of the rain, there was mud everywhere, I lied.

It's strange to see you in running gear, he said, laughing, before inviting me to join them for breakfast.

I've already had breakfast, I lied again. I'll go have a shower. I'll see you later.

And as I was walking towards the lift, the receptionist called out my name and said that they'd found me another room.

I thought for a moment. A couple of seconds. And then I said that it was OK. That they didn't have to move me to another room. That I would prefer to stay where I was.

14.

I went up into my room and sat on the edge of the bed and looked at the stains. Now I began to look at them differently. Little by little, I began to understand something. Or a part of something.

And it was then that I decided to call a friend of mine who was, who is, a forensic scientist and worked, works, at The National Police Centre in Paris. I'd met her on a course about semiology and the body that we'd both happened to do at the Sorbonne a couple of years previously. She was quite high up in the police force, as criminologists go. For reasons that should be obvious, I can't tell you her real name. For the purposes of this account, we shall call her Marlowe.

I called her and as soon as she picked up, I began to explain why I was calling. I told her about the stains and that I was curious to know what had happened. She suggested we Skype later that evening, after midnight, when she'd be home and free to talk.

15.

After ending my phone call with Marlowe, I went to the University to listen to some of the talks that were being presented at the symposium.

There was one talk that I found particularly interesting. It was a presentation by a colleague from the University of Lisbon on the subject of the myth of Odysseus and the Sirens.

While I was listening to her talk, I found myself asking anew the same question that I always think about whenever I encounter this episode of the Odyssey, namely, what is it that the Sirens actually say to

Odysseus? What do they sing? What is it that he is so desperate to hear that he will risk everything?

At the end of the talk, I went up to her and asked her if we might have lunch together. I was very interested in the topic and I wanted to invite her to contribute to a magazine that I was involved in the publishing of, that was a shared project between my university in Paris and the University of Madrid.

A few hours later, we were having lunch. We'd been joined by several other colleagues, and throughout the meal all we did was discuss her talk. At a certain moment, towards the end of lunch, I mentioned that a poet from my country of origin had written a great poem about Odysseus and the Sirens. And I explained that the poem recounted how Odysseus had tied himself to the mast of his boat, but had desired that the wind would free him. And then I started to recite the poem. In the middle of Ljubljana I began to recite a poem by Idea Vilariño.

But aren't you French?

Yes. Yes. I am. I choose to be French. But I wasn't born in France. I'm French by adoption.

And you were born in Montevideo?

Yes. In Montevideo.

Montevideo is a beautiful name for a city, someone said.

And then I began to explain to them what I have explained to countless others. That maybe Montevideo was called Montevideo because it was the sixth mountain up the river from East to West.

In Nautical terms.

Monte.

VI

d.

E-O

And then I followed that up with what I always follow that up with, which is that the city where I was born was also the birth city of Lautréamont. This was always a surprise to everyone. Especially when I would then explain that his name was actually an homage to the city itself. It was an abbreviation of L'autre à Montevideo. The other in Montevideo.

And then I would always use that revelation to start talking about Lautremont's writing and leave Montevideo behind.

He doesn't like to speak about the country of his birth, someone said.

It's true. I don't like to.

Why?

That's a very personal question, I replied laughing.

Because it was true, I didn't like it when someone asked me why. In fact, I'd have been happier if we'd spoken about whether it was my first time in Ljubljana, or if I preferred smoked salmon that came from Norway or Scotland.

What about this thing I read that you wanted to be a famous singer? I read it in an article. That you always wanted to be a famous singer?

Yes. It's true. I replied.

And it was true. Even as a child, I'd always wanted to be a famous singer. A Frank Sinatra. Or a Nat King Cole. Or Bing Crosby. Or Barry Manilow. I've always wanted to be a star. I've always wanted to fill stadiums. That's what I've always wanted. But whenever I've told anyone this, they act all surprised. I've never understood why. I've never thought it was a strange thing to want.

A singer?

Yes. I've always wanted to be a famous singer. Unfortunately I have a terrible singing voice.

16.

That night, when I got back to my hotel room, I switched on the TV and saw that Godard's *Breathless* was on. I'd never seen it before. Immediately, I was stunned by Jean-Paul Belmondo's beauty in that film. I could never have imagined that he was so good-looking as a young man. And the way he. That incredible way he. Of. His thumb sliding horizontally across his lips.

Like this.

As though with just his thumb, he could end language forever. As though, with just that gesture, he could express everything that had ever needed to be expressed without resorting to words.

So I went to get a Coke and I sat in bed and I dedicated myself to observing Belmondo's sublime body. Especially his torso. Perfect. Extraordinary. But still nothing compared to that gesture of his thumb on his lips.

This one. Like this.

And so I repeated it several times trying to mimic him. And as I was doing so I thought to myself that if anyone in the future ever asked me about my country of origin, I would reply with this gesture.

Like this.

And as I was waiting for the clock to strike 12, and Marlowe's call, I repeated it again and again. And, little by little, I started to imagine that my lips were Igor's.

17.

When the film ended, I looked at the time and saw that I still had an hour and a half until Marlowe would call.

So I thought I could use the time to go over the second section of my talk.

I sat down at the desk, opened my computer, and this time I chose to read it out loud to try to memorise it. It was the section that I knew least well.

The second reason that Narcissus's gaze acts as a metaphor for the artist's gaze is that, I believe, in the same way that his gaze ends up producing a transformation, the gaze of the artist is a gaze that transforms reality. Narcissus, through his gaze, transforms into something else, into something vegetable, into the flower that carries his name. And this capacity that his gaze has to transform, to transmute, to convert, to transfigure one thing into another, is what I would define as the poetic capacity that the artist draws upon to transform one thing into another. It is what transforms windmills into giants; the very act of looking incites a change in reality that will then forever be other. The transformation of one thing into an other is precisely the job of the poet. Heidegger, when explaining what he would classify as poetic production, affirms and insists upon the quality of transformation, stating that what is occurring is a process by which something escapes its original state to change itself into something else, thus generating a new / entity.

Suddenly the phone rang. It was Igor. He was calling from the hotel lobby.

Can I come up?

I told you I didn't want us to see each other here. Plus, I've got lots of work.

We can be quick.

OK. But no drugs. I've only got an hour.

Five minutes later, he in was in my room.

18.

I shut the door and right away we began to undress each other furiously and fuck. Not a word had been spoken. We'd not even said hello. We fucked all over the room.

After a while, I looked at the time on my watch and I realised that an hour had already passed.

Do you never take it off?, he asked me. When you make love, do you never take it off?

I don't know. I've never thought about it. I've never asked myself that question.

What kind of watch is it?

It's a Casio.

Is it waterproof or water-resistant?

OK. OK. It's waterproof to 50 metres. It's got a stopwatch and an alarm clock… This is strange. Anyway, it's time that you left.

You don't like being with me.

No. It's not that. If I didn't like being with you, you wouldn't be here. Here. Now. Naked.

I want us to fuck again, he insisted. I like how hard you make me.

I like it too. But I can't now. I'm waiting for a phone call from a colleague. It's important.

And so we began to get dressed. And as we did so, I couldn't take my eyes off him, I couldn't not watch him. Not even for a second did I stop watching him as he recovered his body. I couldn't stop watching how he pulled up his trousers with both hands. I watched the strong muscles of his forearms tense up one last time as he pulled his trousers over his sex with one sharp movement. Then I watched him pull at his belt, pull it through the clasp, and tighten it shut. I watched him looking at himself in the mirror, checking that everything was perfect. I watched him button up his shirt. And then I watched him bend down to put on his Adidas trainers and tie the shoelaces in a tight double bow. And finally, I watched him stand up straight and perform the last act of this ceremonial re-dressing, as he put his right hand into his trousers to accommodate his sex.

It was obvious he liked to show himself off. And be watched. He was magnificent and he knew it. He knew it better than anyone.

You like it, I said to him as he wet his hair and combed it back with his fingers.

What?

That people watch you.

He took a Coke out of the minibar, drank it in one go, and left.

19.

When I went back to my desk I noticed that Marlowe had just come online. Two minutes later, she called me on Skype.

Can you hear me? Can you see me? And now? OK.
Great. Yes. I can hear you and see you.

So I began to tell her once again the story of the stains, but
almost immediately she stopped me and asked me to show
her them. Like any good criminologist, Marlowe wasn't
into small talk. Her thing was to look at the concrete facts
and not waste time on platitudes.

I'll show you them on my iPhone.

And that's what I did. What I'm doing now. I brought up
the camera and began to show her the stains.

I started with the first one I'd noticed and then I showed
her the ones nearest to it. I moved the bed and showed her
the enormous stain that was under the bed.

And I zoomed in and out to give Marlowe a sense of the
size of each stain.

Very quickly, she asked me to get as close as I could and
zoom in on the edges of each stains and trace them all way
round.

Then she asked me to go back to a particular stain and
focus more closely.

OK. So that's the only stain that isn't a blood stain.

It isn't?

No. It looks like it but it isn't. It must be some sort of dark
oil or some sort of sauce. Maybe soya sauce. Soya sauce
looks a lot like blood when it dries.

Then I showed her the stains on the wall. And we went
through the whole procedure once again. I was following
her instructions while he was looking at the evidence and
writing down notes in a little notepad.

After a while, she began to tell me to move around the room. I did as I was told. I obeyed her every instruction. And wherever she told me to go, there were new stains that had been scrubbed at but not completely removed. It was as if Marlowe knew exactly where they were going to be. And so, little by little, she made me realise that there were many many more stains in the room than I had realised. On the walls, in the hallway, on the cupboard walls, on the table legs of the desk.

Then she asked me to film the ceiling.

The ceiling?

Yes. The ceiling.

And yes, there they were. On the ceiling, you could just about make out tiny little specks of blood. A constellation of blood stains. A fresco of badly scrubbed blood flecks.

Marlowe wasn't explaining a thing. She looked and took notes. That was all.

Then she asked me to trace a journey with the camera that she would explain to me. So I started filming in the hallway, moving into the bathroom, and when I got to the bathroom, I realised that there were lots of barely visible blood stains in there too. On the walls, on the floor, on the ceiling, in the bathtub itself. There were a lot of stains in the bath.

It was again as if Marlowe had already understood what had happened. As if she knew how this story ended.

She asked me to get a swab of cotton and to rub it against one of the stains.

I did so. I did what she asked.

Like this?

Yes. Just like that.

The cotton had turned a faint pinkish red. I zoomed in.

And now?

Marlowe asked me to wet it with some alcohol.

I told her I didn't have any.

She told me to get a miniature whisky out of the minibar.

I did as she asked and upon wetting the cotton, the colour became much darker and more intense. It became red again. The alcohol was bringing out the original colour of the stain.

It's exactly as I thought, said Marlowe. What I need you to do now is to take some measurements.

OK, I said, and I began to measure with my fingers the distances that Marlowe wanted to look at. Distances between one stain and another. Distances between the stains on the floor and the stains on the walls. Distances between the stains in the bath and those on the bathroom door.

OK, she said after a while. That's all. It's obvious what happened.

Marlowe asked me to stop and sit down. And then she said.

What happened here was horrific.

A murder, right?, I asked her.

Something much worse. A dismemberment. The victim's major limbs were cut off and possibly other parts too. A very dark thing happened here. Why don't you leave?

But what actually happened?, I asked.

I don't know for sure, said Marlowe. What I can tell you is that given the types of stain, the pattern and location of the stains and the distances between them, the dismembering was achieved with a knife. There was no bullet, that's obvious. But there are the sprayed teardrop-shaped stains and splatter patterns that are consistent with the dismembering of a body with a knife, and probably a serrated knife at that.

And all of that happened here?

It probably all took place on the floor by the bed and then in the bathroom. Given the visible traces, the first incisions almost certainly took place by the bed, but it's also clear that new incisions were also made in the bathroom. And given the splatter pattern, it looks likely that the victim's organs were removed. That almost certainly happened in the bathroom.

The body was massacred.

No. Massacred, no. That would have left different traces and different marks. The victim's body was dismembered. It's different. Why don't you leave the room?

The hotel's full, I lied.

Why don't you go to another hotel?

How can I find out what actually happened?, I asked her again.

That's the only thing you're interested in. I don't know. Someone at the hotel must know what happened. If I were in your shoes, I'd leave now.

Don't worry.

One thing. If you are going to write about this, could you please change my name? I could get into trouble.

Don't worry. I'd already planned on doing that. I'm going to call you Marlowe.

Like Shakespeare's rival.

No. Marlowe like Philip Marlowe. The detective in
Raymond Chandler's novels.

20.

Having thanked her and said goodbye, I hung up and
sat at the desk for a few minutes, repeatedly scanning the
entire room.

Marlowe was right, the only thing that interested me was
knowing what had happened in the room. But it wasn't
just a question of personal curiosity. No. It was more of a
professional defect, I thought to myself as I selected one of
Bach's Cello Suites to listen to. I needed to hear something
beautiful.

The room was now a huge mess and my thoughts were
just as confused. I didn't want to put everything back in
order. All I wanted to do was lie down on the floor. Here.
Just here. Right on top of where the biggest stain was. Here
where it had all started. Or all ended. Here. Right here.
It was the only thing I wanted to do. To lie down on the
carpet and listen to Bach.

Why did I no longer want to leave? Why did I feel such
increasing desire to be here where such a horrific bloody
crime had taken place? Why did I feel so drawn to this
room?

And as I began to fall asleep, some verses by Idea Vilariño
sprang to my mind.

I say no

I say no

As I cling to the mast

And yet

Hoping the wind brings it down

That the siren with her teeth

Cuts the ropes and pulls me down, down

Saying no no no

But following her.

21.

That whole night, I dreamed of Igor.

When I woke up the next morning, I wanted to see him. I thought about calling him, but then I decided not to.

I went running, excited by the thought that I might come upon Igor in the Tivoli Park. This time I ran looking around me. Looking for him in amongst the trees. Looking for him in the bushes at the side of the path. As my legs became more and more tired and I began to sweat, I still couldn't stop looking from side to side. I couldn't see him anywhere. It was early, so early that I alone was out.

Where are you? I was thinking. All the time, Where are you?

The sun began to rise.

All I wanted to do was see him. To caress him. That he should be waiting for me, his body as sweaty as mine was, his long hair, wet. That was all I wanted that morning. That he should beckon me to come to him from some hidden place.

His image was all I had in my mind. I couldn't think about my talk. Nor anything else.

And then, out of nowhere, I thought of writing this play. This exact scene. Then that was all that I could think about. Writing a new play. A play in which I myself would be telling the story. A play about the hotel and the stains, about Narcissus and the conference, about Igor and running, about talking to my mum on Skype and refugees drowning, of Belmondo and Lautremont, of Bach and and Bowie. A play where, little by little, everything begins to blur together. A play that takes place in my room. My hotel room where I practice my talk. Where I can talk about my encounters with Igor. Where I start to cohabit with the stains of a dismemberment whose origins I, slowly but surely as the play goes on, begin to uncover. A play that slowly begins to reconstruct the crime scene itself.

And just as I was thinking all these thoughts, that's when I saw him. Him. Igor.

He was exactly as I'd hoped. Exactly as I had imagined him in my mind's eye. As though there was no Igor. As though he was only a figment of my imagination. And yet, there he was. In front of me.

I knew I'd meet you here. I knew you'd be somewhere near the lake.

And then he did Belmondo's gesture.

This one.

The exact same gesture.

Now, he was doing that gesture to me. It wasn't Belmondo or me. It was him. It might seem strange, but it wasn't. When you write, things can shift. Now, the gesture was his. It had become his.

And it was then, at that exact moment, that I thought of Sam. Sam Crane.

It was at that exact moment that he thought about me and that it would be amazing if this gesture that I'm doing right now could be shared amongst the four of us. Belmondo. Igor. Him. Me.

31

And so that's what we did. Right there. We took ourselves off to a clearing, hidden away amongst the poplars and we began to do it. And as we were doing it, there were the four of us. The four of us doing it. The four of us doing it amongst ourselves.

Me.

Him.

Igor.

Belmondo.

When you write, everything is permissible. Or, almost everything.

And that was when, exactly where he'd had the idea, Sergio decided to call me.

22.

Sam, Hi.

Hey… You OK?

I'm calling from Ljubljana.

From where?

From Ljubljana.

What?

It's a capital city. It's the capital of Slovenia.

I know. But.

I'm calling you because I want to tell you something. A new idea. A new play. A new project that I would like for us to do together. And… That's all I wanted to say. When I get back to the hotel, I'll send you an email and I'll tell you more.

Great. I'll be waiting. You know the answer is going to be yes.

OK then. I'll catch you / later.

Sergio. Wait. I also have something to tell you. Something very important. Nobody else knows yet.

I'll guess. You're having another baby.

Yes. How did you know?

It doesn't matter. How are you feeling?

I… I don't know… I just… Three kids is…

Come on, don't be gay. In theatre, everything works better in threes. It stands to reason the same is true of life.

Don't tell anyone.

No one. Cross my heart and hope to die.

You're an atheist.

I'm in the middle of a park. If I speak a word, I'll hang myself from a tree.

Jesus Christ, Sergio!

The only thing is, for this play, you're going to have to grow your hair long.

Is it another one of your auto-fictions?

I'll tell you later.

So I'm going to be you.

No. No. Not me. You'll be a character version of me. It's different.

First, Trevor White. Now me. Every time, it's someone younger.

I hadn't thought about it that way. You're right. Maybe I'm channelling my inner Dorian Gray.

I've never read it.

Haven't you? You should. In the prologue, there's one of the most beautiful things ever said about art. Something along the lines of 'all art is perfectly useless'.

I don't think that's true.

I know. It's your only fault. I do. I'm convinced that art is completely useless. Anyway, I'll write as soon as I get back to the hotel. A kiss.

Another.

23.

As soon as I hung up, I thought about Sam having a third child. It's strange. It was strange. Just as I had decided to write a play for him, he had told me he was going to have another child. I don't know. There was something about it that struck me as strange.

The sun was beginning to rise above the woods and the fog was lifting.

I suddenly felt good. Sam had said yes. And that was what was most important for me at that moment. That he'd accepted. That he'd said yes. It had been some time that I'd only be able to write about real people. People who actually existed. For real. As if my writing had suddenly begun to need real existences.

Sam had just said yes. That he was up for it. And that made me happy. My heart was filled with joy.

And I thought about a song, a Nat King Cole song. A song that's about all of this. It's called Nature Boy. And well. I'd like to sing it because it's relevant to all of this.

Music, please.

It's a song that I'd like to dedicate to all of you, but most of all to Sam Crane, wherever you may be…

24.

That whole morning, I found it hard to follow the conference. I couldn't concentrate. All I could think of was Igor and the bloodstains.

Without anyone knowing it, I was online looking for images of dismemberments and at the same time, texting Igor.

And so the images of sawn off limbs that were appearing on my iPhone became interspersed with Igor's naked body. He liked to send me photos of himself. Photos of his cock, of his torso. He was aroused that I was looking at them during the conference.

That was what was arousing him. And me too.

Suddenly, I felt an urge to call him.

Where are you?, he asked.

I'm in the theatre… No, at the university. Yes. Yes. I am aroused. Of course I am.

Igor always wanted to know if I was aroused.

What exactly do you want to know? Yes, I'm hard. I'm really big.

And then Igor asked me to go to the toilets and masturbate. He wanted us to masturbate at the same time.

Now?

Yes. Now. Right now. He ordered me.

He loved to give me orders and I loved to obey. To obey him. To be obedient. I loved to submit myself to his every whim.

Yes, that's what I'm saying, that I like obeying you. What? Now?

So I went, I went to lock myself inside one of the toilets and we did it by telephone.

What else? I asked him. What else do you want me to do to you?

As soon as we were done, he began to ask when would see each other again.

Not tonight, no. I can't. Tomorrow I'm giving my talk and I need to concentrate.

And so I tried to explain to him that once I'd given my talk we were going to be able to do anything we wanted.

But he wouldn't have any of it. He told me he had a dealer who could get us some really good stuff.

I know. I know. But not tonight. Tomorrow we can fuck all you like.

We could see each other tomorrow morning in the park.

No. Not in the park. Don't come tomorrow. I would prefer it if we saw each other in the evening at the hotel.

Finally I hung up and I switched my phone off to be able to concentrate on the conference.

25.

That afternoon when I returned to the hotel, they told me that the hotel director was waiting for me in his office. The truth was that I had asked to talk to him.

As soon as he saw me, he jumped up, held out his hand and beckoned me to come into his office.

My name is Zdenko Vladislav, he said.

Actually. Can I just… I'd like to ask your very special permission. I'm not really an actor. The only time I've acted was with my sister in a show called Ostia. I am a writer and a director. What I do is write plays and direct them. But tonight I'd very much like to play Zdenko, the hotel director, for you. Is that OK? Good.

After we'd entered his office and sat down, I began to explain to him the reason why I'd asked to see him, and after listening to me quite carefully, Zdenko asked for my forgiveness and then stated that, in effect, something terrible had happened in my hotel room

A crime, right?

Correct, he replied.

I told him that I'd started my own investigation.

He again asked for my forgiveness and confessed that I was the first person to have been given the room to stay in since the crime had occurred and the ensuing cordoning off by the police. He once again offered to move me to another room with immediate effect.

I told him no.

He was clearly put out. He proceeded to explain to me that he'd followed all the procedural stipulations of the Slovenian police force, that's to say: the sealing up of the room while the police investigation was ongoing and when clearance was given and the room returned to management, that they had followed all the sanitisation requirement stipulated by law, including disinfection, deep cleaning and restoring the room to its original state. All the while, he wouldn't stop begging my forgiveness. He offered to refund me my stay.

I told him no. That that wasn't what I wanted. Especially as I wasn't paying for the room in the first place.

I just want one thing, I said. One thing.

And then I told him what I wanted.

The only thing I want is for you to tell me what happened. That's what I want to know. What happened? How exactly did it happen? When did it happen? Who was the victim? Who the perpetrator?

Zdenko explained to me that for obvious reasons he was unable to give me further details. That the hotel had a client privacy policy and he couldn't break it.

I told him it was very important for me. That I needed to know.

He suddenly looked at me with suspicion and asked if I was part of the French police investigation force.

I told him no. That that was ridiculous. Why on earth would the French police be interested in this story?

The victim was a French national, he told me, and for weeks on end, right up until the case was closed, the French police had come to the hotel again and again.

Well, no I'm not a policeman.

Then why are you so interested?

I don't know. I've been staying in the room. It's understandable that I'd be curious.

You're a professor, right?

Yes. I'm a professor. But I also write.

Ah, you're a writer?

Yes, I write.

What do you write?

What do I write? Well, this, for example. This conversation, for example. I could write it.

I wouldn't want to end up in a book, he said laughing.

Don't worry. You won't. Not in a book. And anyway, I'll change it. I promise. I'll move some things around. For example, instead of you being a woman, I'll make you a man. And besides, I'm not interested in you but in what you're going to tell me. What I want to know is what happened. How did it happen? Who was involved?

That's when he suggested we should meet somewhere other than the hotel. Here, he couldn't talk. Somewhere else, he could. And so he suggested we meet tomorrow, after my talk, in a café called Café Babel.

Does that sound good?

I said that it did. That that was perfect for me.

We both stood up and as we were shaking hands, he asked me to come alone to the café.

Of course, I replied.

Listen, he asked me, you're not related to the young man?

To who?

To the victim?

No. No. Not at all. Was he a young man?

Well, I guess that depends. He was in his early forties.

Is that young?, I asked, laughing.

And she laughed too.

Now I knew a little more. I knew that the stains were from the blood of a French man in his early forties.

26.

I returned to my room, took a shower and then called room service and ordered some sushi.

Two temakis. Two makis. Eight sashimi. Room 228.

And while I was waiting for my food to be brought up, I switched on the TV and started watching a documentary about global warming on National Geographic.

I only had to watch ten minutes to realise that everything is going to end much quicker than we thought. The melting of the ice caps was accelerating at a terrifying rate and there was nothing we could do. Nothing at all. It was already too late.

When the sushi arrived, I switched channels and started to eat my sushi in front of the news that Liverpool had won their Champions League semi-final against Barcelona, the moon was shrinking as it cooled, and San Francisco had become the first city to vote to ban the use of facial recognition. What strange times we lived in.

And then as I was reaching for the remote control, I knocked over the little plastic pot of soya sauce that had come with the sushi, and it landed on the floor by the bed.

I immediately tried to clean up the mess, but it wouldn't come out. The stain wouldn't go.

There.

There was no way to get rid of it.

I went to the bathroom, wet a towel with hot soapy water, but no, it wouldn't come out.

It was a real shame to have stained such a clean carpet. I promised myself that I would tell the cleaners the following morning. They would have some sort of product to remove the stain.

27.

Then my Skype rang. It was my mum. I didn't want to answer but I hadn't spoken to her in two days and it was time, so I did.

Hello. Mum. Can you see me? Hang on? And now? Can you hear me? How are you? What? No. It's me Mum. I'm in Ljubljana. Do you remember I told you that I was in Ljubljana? Yes. It is far away. Yes. What time is it where you are? Yes. You do know how to tell the time. Try. Here it's late. No, don't touch anything. Just talk to me. I don't know. Is there anything you want to tell me? No? OK. This! This morning I heard a Japanese folktale. Here. I'll tell you it. A samurai is standing in front of a mirror with his eyes closed. His wife, on seeing him, approaches him and asks him what he's doing. He replies, I am trying to see how I will look when I am dead. It's good, isn't it? What? No. No, I'm not in Japan. I'm in Slovenia. Near Venice. I told you that already. Do you remember? Mum. Mum. Mum. OK. I'll call you tomorrow.

After hanging up, I got into bed, took my anti-depressants, a sleeping pill, and was lucky to fall asleep straightaway.

28.

The next morning I woke up very early. It was Friday. The day of my talk.

I thought about going running but not in the park. I wanted to go over my speech one last time, and if I was to meet Igor, I wasn't going to be able to.

The best thing was going to be to run in the opposite direction. That's what I'd decided as I left the hotel. Ten minutes later, I realised I was back amongst the poplar trees, and five minutes after that, I felt Igor appear at my side.

I told you I didn't want to do anything this morning. That I wanted to run alone.

He said that he just wanted to run with me. Just run.

OK. But no talking. Not a word.

And so we ran in silence. Together. At the same pace. With the same rhythm. The only thing I could hear was his breath. Nothing else.

After a while, we stopped to drink some water.

Where is it?, he asked.

What?

Your talk.

Why do you want to know?

To know.

I asked him not to come. I didn't want him there. If I saw him there, it would make me feel uncomfortable.

And it was then, for the very first time, just then, that I noticed there was something strange about Igor.

What is it?, he asked, with a frown.

Nothing, I said, all the while thinking to myself, again for the very first time, Who was Igor, really? Why was he so adamant we see each other every day? What did he really want?

He wanted to kiss me.

I said no. I didn't want to get aroused.

Just kiss.

No, I said. I have to go on. I can't get distracted.

And then I told him that I was going to put my headphones in and that I'd rather continue on my own.

He said he would follow behind me. He liked to watch me run in front of him.

OK.

Shall we see each other tonight?

I'll call you when the conference is over.

I put my headphones in. Put Bach's Cello Suites on, and I ran for another half hour, with Igor a couple of metres behind me for the entire time.

Who was Igor really?

What did he want? It was obvious that he wanted more than just to fuck. What could it be? It wasn't money. No. But it was clear that there was something he wanted. Something else.

It was all I thought about as I ran back to the hotel through the centre of the city.

At the corner of the street where the hotel was, we waved goodbye and I went in.

29.

After going up to my room, I had a shower and began to dress in front of the mirror, trying on two or three of the shirts I had brought while deciding on my Kenzo suit. After I'd put on my Casio watch, I stopped for a moment to look at the almost imperceptible lines that were tracing their fragile grooves across my face.

43

How fast everything goes! I thought.

Afterwards I took a taxi and went to the university.

30.

I arrived and went straight to the lecture hall where I was
speaking, and as I waited, watching the room fill up with
over a thousand people, I spotted Igor come in and sit
down at the back. I'd known that he would come.

It doesn't matter, I said to myself.

And so I began my talk.

The first part went brilliantly, to perfection. That was the
part where I spoke about Narcissus's gaze being an inward
gaze, that focused in on itself while searching for the
other. In the second part, however, I felt a little unsettled,
because I hadn't been clear enough in the unfolding of
my argument. That was the part in which I posited the
idea that the artist's gaze, by the act of looking, was itself
transformative. But the third part was great. The third part
was only three minutes long and it was where I justified
my theory that Narcissus's gaze acts as a metaphor for the
artist's gaze.

31.

The third reason that I believe that Narcissus's gaze
resembles the artist's gaze is that both gazes not only
transform what is before them, but also immortalise it.
Let us note that Narcissus transforms into a flower that,
according to the myth, is reborn every spring, that's to
say, a flower that will be immortalised in perpetual vernal
rebirth. We therefore have before us an auto-generative
botanical species that never dies. That capacity for
immortalisation through the gaze is a perfect metaphor

for the gaze of the artist, creator, poet, for he or she also immortalises their creation. And if we take this thought further, the artist becomes immortal too. This makes me think of something that Deleuze maintained when he stated that art is an act of resistance. Because he's not talking about political or social resistance, but of metaphysical resistance whereby every work of art is an act of resistance against death. We only need to look upon a three thousand-year-old sculpture or Leonardo's Last Supper to acknowledge that these works have resisted oblivion. I always insist that it's not by pure chance that the very first poem, the very first work of human literary endeavour, the Epic of Gilgamesh, written in cuneiform on those famous clay tablets by an unknown Babylonian author, should have as its principal theme the rejection of death and the quest for immortality. I believe that every poet is deeply afraid of death. 'Must I die too? Anguish gnaws at my insides', says Gilgamesh. And like Gilgamesh, we don't want to die. And so with our gaze, just like Narcissus, we attempt to immortalise, to make oblivion-proof the works we create. And it's not just we poets who are afraid of death, but also those who stand before acts of creation. I am convinced that one of Art's key functions is to suspend, even if just for an instant, our shared terror of dying and that is what, ultimately, makes us beautifully human.

Thank you very much.

32.

After my talk, there was a Q&A with the audience, who asked various questions, including, of course, as you might expect, the moment when Igor put his hand up and asked me why I was so afraid of dying.

I wasn't particularly gracious as I replied that this was a very intimate question and that I wouldn't be able to answer it. That it was very personal.

Several other questions were asked and, as the post-talk debate came to an end, I looked for Igor, but he was no longer there. He had disappeared.

Some colleagues asked me to join them for lunch so that we might continue discussing my talk. I had no burning desire to accept their invitation but I knew I must. I couldn't say no. And in any case, all I had to do was to keep quiet, and just listen. There was always one person who had something interesting to say.

33.

In the end, it was a very pleasant lunch where, on top of receiving the praise of colleagues and invitations to other conferences, I was also able to defend certain positions I had taken in my talk that had raised doubts among my peers.

After dessert, I was a little shocked when a colleague said that it would have been interesting if someone in the Q&A had asked me why I was so afraid of dying.

I was even more shocked when others around the table agreed with him, saying that yes, it would have been interesting if someone had asked me that.

That meant that no one had heard Igor's question. Or worse still, that I alone had. Or even more disturbingly, that Igor hadn't even asked a question. Or worst of all, that Igor hadn't even been there.

Yes, now everything was beginning to shift in very strange ways. Yes, now I had the feeling that things were going to get even stranger.

I suddenly felt a huge pain in my head, right here, and so I took my leave from my colleagues, left the restaurant, called a taxi and went to the meeting I'd arranged at Café Babel.

34.

As we travelled through the city, I looked out of the taxi, and tried to remember the moment in which Igor had asked me that question that no one else had seemed to hear. The memory seemed clear. Sharply focused. I could recall it with absolute clarity.

But what if it was all made up?, I asked myself. Pure imagination and nothing else.

So then I took my iPhone out to check if his name was in it, and if we had indeed texted and called, and just as I was about to do so, the driver broke suddenly and announced that we had arrived.

35.

At a table at the back of the café sat Zdenko with another man. As I walked towards them, they stood up.

This is Piotr Malvec, he said.

I just want to say that Piotr Malvec is the last character we're going to meet tonight.

Piotr Malvec was a recently retired ex-Chief of Police and he had led the investigation into what had happened in room 228, his last case as it turned out. He was no spring chicken and had enjoyed a stellar police career. He'd also been Tito's head of personal security back when Yugoslavia was Yugoslavia. He was clearly an educated man, spoke French fluently and was a reader of Poe, Borges, Stevenson and Mallarmé.

Zdenko had made his acquaintance during the investigation and had decided to contact him so that he might answer some of the questions I had.

What exactly would you like to know?, asked Piotr in perfect French.

Everything, I answered.

Very well, he said, and after a brief look around to check no one was listening, he began to tell his tale with that coldness that comes naturally to those who work with the dead.

I'm going to try to reproduce his account as accurately as possible.

36.

The crime had taken place exactly here. The dismemberment took place on the floor by the bed, in the hallway, and in the bathroom. The body had been cut up into tiny pieces so that it could be removed from the hotel without anyone realising. The crime had been committed by one person acting alone. A man in his mid-thirties.

And the weapon, I asked Piotr.

An electric knife, he answered. A Moulinex to be precise.

After that, all the while that Piotr was telling me how the body had been cut up with the electric knife, the only thing I could think of was the sound.

Listen.

I want to you to imagine the sound of the knife. Imagine it cutting through skin. Through nerves. Through veins and arteries. Then through the tendons. The tendons and then through the bones. Cutting and sawing through bone.

And the worst of it, if what Piotr was telling me was true, was that the victim had still been alive while his body was being destroyed. Given the results of the forensic tests, the intensity of the impact of the stains on the walls, it had been concluded that the victim had witnessed his own dismemberment. He had seen how it had happened. His body had only expired a few minutes after his limbs had been cut off. He'd had time enough to observe the separation of his body and each limb, one by one.

Once the body was lifeless, the murderer had spent a good while cutting up the torso, starting by opening up the sternum and sawing through the ribs before dragging it to the bathroom where he'd emptied it of its organs. The lungs, the liver, the kidneys, the heart.

Once done, he'd gathered all the body parts and put them in a large Adidas hold-all in order to carry the body out of the hotel without anyone noticing.

The police had taken days to recover the body. The murderer had discarded all the body parts throughout Tivoli Park, except for the victim's head. That he placed in a cardboard box and sent first class to the Philology Department of the University of Ljubljana.

Piotr had then confessed that at the autopsy, it hadn't been easy for any of those present to face the victim's cut up body. According to Piotr, they'd had to stop a number of times.

The worst had been the head, he'd told me. The victim's features were completely unrecognisable due to the bashing in the face had taken.

The autopsy report was more precise in its description.

Skull features multiple fractures and various caving in of bone. Nasal cartilage has moved upwards into the cranium.

The jaw bone is lacerated. Presence of extensive bruising, contusions and swelling.

Piotr also told me how they thought the murderer had created such damage to the skull. They thought he'd grabbed the head and smashed it on one of the corners of the desk. At least three times.

I'd like you to please imagine what that would have been like.

One. Two. Three.

37.

Piotr didn't just tell me all of this, he'd also brought the crime scene photos, the summary of the forensic report, and a couple of apples.

They're Slovenian he said. Our national pride. Our main export industry. We're Europe's leading apple exporter.

Having spent a couple of hours in Café Babel, we left and walked through the streets of Ljubljana. After some time, just before we said goodbye, Piotr asked me if I was going to write about all of this.

I said that I didn't know.

You've got the most extraordinary job in the world, he said. I've always admired those incapable of living in the real world. This need to confuse everything. To mix truth and fiction. To live with that which is imaginary.

We reached a corner and I asked him a final question.

And the motive for the crime?

It was never very clear, he answered. As we never caught the murderer, we can only speculate. There are three possibilities, each as likely or unlikely as each other. The first possibility is document trafficking, we never found the victim's ID documents and ID trafficking is both popular and lucrative here in Slovenia. The second possibility is organ trafficking. We never recovered any of the victim's organs and again, organ trafficking is a very lucrative business in this part of the world.

And the third possibility.

Rage. Yes. Pure and simple rage. Fury. Anger. An explosion. A momentary fury is all it takes to kill someone is much simpler than people think. It's something we're all capable of.

But then, to cut the body up into a thousand pieces with an electric knife?

Well, it's not that complicated to understand either. If the rage is all consuming and the knife is sharp, then it's only a matter of strength and precision. Nothing more.

He stretched out his arm and hailed a cab. Before getting in, Piotr held out his hand, and as we shook, he leaned in and quietly he said: the word rage is beautiful is it not? A good word for a title, don't you think? The Rage of... actually, what did you come to the conference to speak about?

About Narcissus. About the myth of Narcissus.

Well, there you have it. The Rage of Narcissus. There's your title. It's a good title.

And then they got into the cab and left.

I stood for a minute thinking about everything he'd told me, and then I started to make my way back to the hotel with his apples in my hands.

38.

When I got back to the room, I sat on the edge of the bed and I stayed like that for a couple of seconds, unable to not think about what Piotr had just told me.

All of a sudden, I felt scared. But it was late. It was already too late.

I didn't feel like going to the end of conference dinner. Instead I grabbed one of the apples and began to eat it.

This apple was going to be my last meal. My last me/

The phone rang. It was Igor. He wanted to see me. He was inviting me to go to a private party in the suburbs of the city.

I told him that I didn't much feel like going out.

He insisted. He said that there were going to be thirty men there. You'll like them all.

I don't know if I want to be with lots of men, I said.

The other day you said you liked it.

Yes. I do. But I don't feel like going out tonight.

The sex will be great. The drugs will be great.

Igor began to text me photos. It was impossible to not get excited. It was impossible to say no.

Half an hour later Igor arrived in a taxi, I went down to meet him, and we took off for the suburbs.

39.

It was huge house with a swimming pool.

The guy whose party it was played for the Slovenian national football team, and everyone else was either a sportsperson or a porn actor.

There were about thirty men in different rooms all over the whole house. In the swimming pool, there was already a group fucking.

I'm guessing you know how this works, asked Igor.

I looked at him and told him that I lived in a city unparalleled for its excesses.

The ritual of these events was always the same. Everyone could take whatever they wanted to take and do whatever they wanted with whomever they chose to do it with.

We started out together walking through the house, fucking this person and then that person, and then fucking in threes, and fours, and then with whomever and however many who wanted to join in.

The idea was to keep things moving. To try new things. To mix and combine and look for different combos. To watch and be watched. To try out different people, different bodies, different groups.

In some rooms, it was so dark, we didn't even know who we were fucking.

And that's how we spent the whole night. Always searching for more. That each experience should be more intense, more engaging, more arousing. As if nothing could bring us back down. As if nothing could satiate us.

At one point, I realised seven hours had passed by since we'd arrived. The sun was rising.

With everything we've done, it's no surprise that we've lost track of time.

I know, I answered. Why don't we go? We can go back to my hotel and fuck there?

So we called a taxi, left and went back together to the hotel.

We had all day to fuck. My flight wasn't leaving till the next morning. Now we were going to be able to do whatever we wanted without having to pretend anything to anyone.

As the taxi snaked through the city, we spoke not a word to each other. We didn't even look at each other. We were crashing hard.

All of a sudden, blood began to trickle down from one of my nostrils.

I took a lot.

It's nothing, said Igor, handing me a kleenex.

And I leaned my head on his shoulder and we stayed like that, silent, for the rest of the taxi journey. The only thing we wanted was to go back to fucking, in spite of the tiredness in our bones.

40.

We got back to my room, I locked the door with a key and we began to fuck again as we had fucked many times before.

At one point, Igor got up, said that he would only be a moment, and went to the bathroom to have a shower.

I got up too to get myself a Coke and that's when, for the first time, I had a look inside his Adidas holdall which he'd left open. I was surprised to notice that it looked like there was an electric kitchen knife inside. A Moulinex. I opened the bag a little to see if I'd seen right and just as I did, Igor came out of the bathroom.

What's that, I asked him, pointing inside the bag.

Nothing, replied Igor, as he took my iPhone, flicked through my music library, and selected the first track he could find. He put it up to full volume. It was Bach's Cello Suite. It's nothing.

Yes. It's a knife. It's an electric kitchen knife.

And?

Well, it's strange.

And why are you going through my things?

I wasn't going through your things. I was just getting a Coke and I noticed there was a knife in your bag.

As I was trying to explain, Igor came towards me and faster than a blur grabbed me by the neck, like this, with one of his hands.

What's going on?, I said, just as Bach's cellos began to fill the entirety of the room.

Nothing, he said. Nothing at all.

But Igor's grip was getting tighter and tighter.

You're hurting me, I said.

And his left hand came up to join his right hand and he began to tighten his hold with both hands at the same time.

It hurts. I can't breathe.

His face was different. It wasn't the face I knew.

What are you doing? What are you doing?

Igor was strangling me harder and harder and not saying a word.

I'd thought it was a joke at first, but I was beginning to understand that he wanted to hurt me. That's when I heard a noise. Here. Just here. As if something was breaking. And I felt a sharp sharp pain that began to rise up here.

You're strangling me, I said, as I felt blood begin to trickle out of my ear. You're killing me.

And that was when, gripping my neck with his strong left hand, he stretched out his right and brought out the knife from the bag. Then he smashed me against the wall.

You're hurting me, I said, struggling to escape his grip.

His face was still changing. It was transforming before my very eyes. It was no longer the same. I kicked out and nothing. He switched on the electric kitchen knife and after showing it to me, he began. He began to move it closer to my body.

No. Don't. That was all I managed to say before the knife came into contact with my arm and he began to cut my arm off.

The only thing that followed was a scream, my scream as I felt the pain of the knife cutting through my skin and then muscle, veins and tendons and nerves.

His face was getting more and more splashed with my blood but he seemed not to notice.

My cries became louder when the knife began to saw through my bones. I was somehow able to watch my arm separate from my shoulder and I saw it fall to the floor. Bach's cellos continued to fill the room.

Suddenly the pain was too much and my legs gave way. I felt Igor's hand on my neck tighten further and something else broke. And then he let go and my body was on the floor.

And it was then that Igor went to work cutting off other parts of me with the knife.

And as it continued, I began to lose my sight. Everything was becoming blurred. Still, I saw him cut off my other arm and push it to one side. And then I watched him start to cut at one my legs. Little by little, everything began to switch off. And then, finally, I felt a surge of blood vomit up my throat, and a few seconds later, as I felt the knife cut into my groin, everything stopped forever.

EPILOGUE

It was three in the afternoon on a Saturday in London when I answered my phone. It was Sergio's sister.

I could hardly make out a word of what she was saying at first. Finally I understood. Something terrible had happened to Sergio.

I didn't know what to say. I said nothing. I could only listen in silence as she told me Sergio was dead.

I wondered if I should call his mother, but she said no. That it was better not to. That the family back home had tried to explain to her what had happened, but she hadn't understood what they were talking about.

It's better like this, she said. It's better she doesn't understand.

All that night, I didn't know what to do. We all called each other. Daniel. Trevor. Alex. Not one of us could believe that it was true. We all thought it was a lie. That it was just another one of Sergio's auto-fictions.

The next morning, Sergio's sister called me again and asked if I would go to Ljubljana. Sergio's family was in Montevideo. His mum was unwell. They couldn't just... Being in London, it was obviously easier for me to get out there. The idea was that I would be present at Sergio's cremation and that I would bring back the ashes, first to London and then eventually to Montevideo.

The next day, I was on a plane to Ljubljana, a city I'd never even really thought about just a few days before.

As I came out of arrivals, there was a man from the embassy waiting for me with a car, and he drove me to a hotel.

This hotel.

This room.

The room was this one. This exact room.

Then I did what I always do when I arrive at a hotel where I am going to be staying for a while. I unpacked my suitcase. I prepared my desk. I plugged in my computer, put my iPhone on charge and I logged onto the wifi with the code they'd given me at reception. I wanted to call home.

Everything was OK. As we were chatting, I noticed Pinny's hand go down to her belly. Here. She'd done it without thinking. When I pointed it out to her, we couldn't stop ourselves from smiling.

The next morning, the same embassy man came to pick me up and he drove me to the crematorium of Ljubljana's central cemetery. The incineration was to take place at ten.

It was all very quick.

They made me go into a room where there was a closed coffin. The room was cold.

I moved towards the coffin and I stood there looking at it for a few minutes.

Eventually my gaze shifted and I noticed a Bible on a small table next to the coffin. It was the only possible source of comfort in the entire room. Even for me, who couldn't believe that anyone could believe. I picked it up and flicked through it. It fell open at the book of Ecclesiastes.

The pages were very worn. They must have been the pages most read in this place. There was a passage marked out in yellow highlighter - 'For the living know they will die; but the dead know nothing, for in the grave, whither thou goest, there is no work, nor device, nor knowledge, nor wisdom'.

Then one of the crematorium employees came up to me and explained in a solemn voice that in two minutes he would be switching on the conveyer belt which would move the coffin into the incinerator.

So now I only had two minutes. I didn't know what to do. I stretched out my hand and placed it on the coffin and I began to caress it as if I was caressing him. I don't like to be caressed, Sergio would always say to me. I don't like being touched. And now that's what I was doing. Now I was moving my hand up and down where I imagined his body to be.

And that was when I saw a metal plate that said:

Sergio Blanco

Montevideo 1976 - Ljubljana 2019

The crematorium assistant moved towards a metal platform where there was an electronic desk with a number of screens and buttons, and after a small nod of the head, he activated the system.

The coffin began to ever so slowly creep its way on the metal conveyor belt and as it approached the wall, with perfect timing, a small shiny metal door slid up to allow the box to enter the oven.

Everything was working to perfection.

Once the coffin was completely inside, the shiny metal door slid back down and the only thing you could hear was the deafening roar of the gas flames bursting into life, deadened by the thickness of the metal walls of the oven.

The assistant once again came up to me and explained that if I wished to see the incineration taking place inside the oven there was a little window on the side for precisely that purpose.

I thought about it for a moment but finally decided that Sergio probably wouldn't have wanted me to. I remembered when we'd gone swimming at the lido the last time he was London, he'd turned away from me as he got undressed. He didn't like to be watched.

Less than half an hour later, the same assistant appeared with an urn and gave it to me. It was still warm. You could still feel the heat within.

After that he asked me to sign some papers, then shook my hand in a very friendly manner and told me I was free to go.

The chauffeur was waiting for me outside the cemetery. I got in the car, and holding the urn in my lap, I asked to be taken back to the hotel.

As soon as I entered the room, I thought to myself that it was strange to be there with Sergio's ashes. We'd been on holiday together a couple of times but we'd never shared a room. This would be the first and last time we shared a room.

Turning around I realised that on the bed lay Sergio's suitcase with all his belongings and on the desk was his computer. I was going to have to take them back with me to London.

Of course, I opened his computer. There was a document open on the desktop. It was the complete text of this play.

I sat up on the bed and began to read. I read it in one go, bristling with envy at not having written it myself. It was perfect, beautiful, brilliant. Like everything Sergio wrote.

When I finished it, I remained still for a moment. Nobody else apart from me knew that this text existed.

I thought about claiming it for myself. I could easily change the name. Remove Sergio Blanco and sign it with Sam Crane. I was tempted, but would anyone believe that I'd written it? I'm not really a writer. I am an actor and a performer.

And then I thought that the best thing to do would be to leave Sergio's name on it but add a prologue and a bit in the middle in which he would say that he'd written the play for me and that he wanted me to perform it.

I sat down at the desk and I began to edit it. I changed a few things, a few dates, little things here and there. In the end, I added quite a lot, a lot more than I thought I was going to add. I made sure my name Sam Crane appeared quite a few times throughout but not too many times, and, when I was happy with all the little modifications I'd made, I exported it to a pdf, closed the computer, and put it into the suitcase.

His final text was now a text that he'd written for me. I liked that. A lot. His last text would be dedicated to me. I would perform it. And I would be brilliant in it. I could already imagine the standing ovations, the incredible reviews, the West End transfer.

As my flight was only leaving much later that evening, I decided to go to the Natural History Museum. The scene that he'd written about the museum seemed to me to be one of the most beautiful passages of the script and I felt a great desire to go there.

I called a taxi.

The museum was completely empty and the rooms were exactly as Sergio had described in his play. I slowly walked through the rooms of vitrines, until I found the stairs to the upstairs galleries and then, suddenly, there he was.

The mammoth.

He was truly huge. And magnificent. Above all, he was magnificent.

Now I understood why Sergio had chosen to call the play The Mammoth's Caress. It was impossible not to feel a sensation of ecstasy before the skeleton of this animal. But that couldn't be the name of the play. The Rage of Narcissus was a much better title. That's why I'd changed it in the text. That's why I'd added that scene with the apples. That's what this play was about. Sergio had transformed himself into another Narcissus who killed himself in his own play. As a champion of auto-fiction he'd managed to take the form to its logical conclusion, textual suicide. The Mammoth's Caress was a good title but The Rage of Narcissus did a better job of conveying the idea of self-murder that took place in the play.

The only rage that Sergio could feel towards anyone was the rage he felt against himself.

I put in my earphones, just as Sergio had asked me to do in his play, and having chosen Bach's Cello Suites, I went closer to the enormous skeleton.

And for the first time, I played being him. For the first time, I tried to be him. For the first time, I was him.

He was immense. Exquisite. A structure of hundreds of graceful bones that rose together in the centre of the room as though a prehistoric cathedral. He was the oldest example found on the continent. I went closer and, without anyone seeing me, I gathered my courage and I brought my hands to him and I began to caress him. I let my hands gently trace every bone. The femurs. The tibias. The ribs. I suddenly felt something in my throat. And then in my chest. Here. Right here. As though for a few seconds something stopped inside me, while I understood somewhere deep down that I was touching something very distant and alien, and at the same time very close and known.

And then I thought about my unborn child who was going to come into this world and I couldn't stop myself from bursting into tears.

There's no more. That's it.

Thank you. Thank you very much.

APPENDIX I

TRANSLATOR'S NOTE

As with my translation and adaptation of *Thebes Land*, I've seen my job as that of translating the experience of Sergio's text over that of translating him word for word. Sergio writes auto-fiction. As he himself explains in this play, he bases his plays on actual lived personal experiences and then uses those experiences as a launchpad for his works of fiction.

To make his plays work in another context, one must do the same. Sergio wrote *La Ira de Narciso* to be performed by Gabriel Calderón in Montevideo in 2014. I have written *The Rage of Narcissus* to be performed by Sam Crane in London in 2019. What happens to Sergio and Gabriel must be reimagined to happen to Sergio and Sam. It cannot be the same. It must not be the same.

Like in Escher's painting, Sergio delights in making possible the impossible. Fact and fiction meet and merge and swim impossibly close together. Like with a mobius strip, he wants us to lose sense of where one ends and the other starts, both of them turning inside out so that they do the work of the other and back again.

He asks one thing of his collaborators (and we are many) and that is that you play the game. You have to put yourself in the play. You have to auto-fictionalise yourself. Maybe there is no Daniel Goldman. Maybe the person whose words you're reading right now is Sergio and I am pretending to be Daniel Goldman, writing these words. Or perhaps better still, maybe there is no Sergio at all. Maybe there is only Daniel Goldman, and Sergio Blanco is a nom-de-plume. Or maybe there is neither Sergio nor Daniel.

Maybe there is only Gabriel and only Sam. Perhaps to be most truthful to Sergio, you have to destroy Sergio.

In any case, I, Daniel, wanted to share certain sections of the original script as I first translated them before the adaptation process began. My reasons are twofold. Firstly, so that you can see what Sergio's play was like in its first incarnation, before the adaptation process began to create ripples. Secondly, so that if you are an artist interested in doing your own version of the play, you can see Sergio's words as he wrote them, before they were transformed and made other by my gaze.

Daniel Goldman
January 2020

APPENDIX II

First translations of *La Ira de Narciso* before the adaptation process began… and where appropriate, notes. Numbers refer to chapters. '…' means that there were no major changes before or after the section that appears.

Cast List

SERGIO BLANCO

GABRIEL CALDERON

—

The original first verse of Fernando Pessoa's poem 'Autopsicografia' is as follows:

> O poeta é um fingidor
> Finge tão completamente
> Que chega a fingir que é dor
> A dor que deveras sente.

—

PROLOGUE

Hello and good evening. I hope you are well. Thank you for being here. Really. Thank you.

Before we start, I'd like to make something clear, which is that I am not Sergio Blanco. My name is Gabriel. Gabriel Calderón. In other words, who you're looking at is not

Sergio Blanco. Or, perhaps a better way of putting it is that this person standing here in front of you is not Sergio Blanco but Gabriel Calderón. I will do everything in my power to be like him. To be him. Well, perhaps not to be him exactly, not Sergio himself, but to be his character, that's to say, to be the character of Sergio. So I will do all I can to be him and I ask of you all that you make the effort to believe that I am him.

One morning last May I received a phone call from Sergio. He was calling from Ljubljana. It was the first time he spoke to me about this piece. It was a very short conversation. Before putting the phone down he told me he would send me an email with more details. Two hours later I switched on my computer and there was an email from Sergio. I opened it with excitement, the excitement I feel every time I open an email from Sergio. In the email, Sergio was asking me to be a part of this piece. It was impossible to say no. That is how all of this began.

I have the email here and I'd like to read it to you.

'My friend, as I just told you on the phone, I am in Ljubljana. I came here to give a conference on Narcissus at the University's Department of Philology. The city is beautiful and the men are amazing. Anyway, I'm writing to you because I'm writing a new play, inspired by this city. It's a fable. I am going to write it for you. Yes. I would like you to be in it. To interpret it. To do it. Everything bar perform it. I propose that we do it next year. I'll direct it. We'll open in Montevideo and then we'll tour it. Minutti hasn't stopped asking me for a new show for next year. Please say yes. If you say no, then I'll stop writing it right now, and then, my life, you will be responsible for its non-existence. A thousand kisses everywhere. I. Sergio.'

8.

When I left the museum, I realised I was hungry and, rather than go through the tiresome process of choosing a restaurant and pointing at a menu and asking questions in a language I didn't speak to a waiter who also didn't speak it about a cuisine that I knew nothing about, I went to the McDonald's across the street.

It was simple, fast and efficient. With just three gestures and a two minute wait, I left the counter with a burger, fries and a Coke.

Having eaten with great discipline every last crumb and every last fry, I walked back to the hotel. I want to do a bit of work on my talk, especially the beginning. I thought it would be best to start by thanking the interpreters who would be simultaneously translating my Spanish into more than twenty languages.

So I opened my computer and began to rewrite the beginning.

~~I would like to thank.~~ I would like to, before I start, begin by offering my thanks to the interpreters for their work and to ask for their forgiveness. With me, they won't be encountering the elegant Castilian of the Iberian peninsula but rather a Spanish that is dry, raw and ~~crude~~. Sorry. It's begun. Crude is a horrible term. Coarse. Coarse is better. Or muddy. A Spanish that is as muddy as the waters of the Rio de la Plata that bathes the banks of Montevideo which is the city where ~~I was born.~~ Sorry. Which is the city where I come from. And to this I will add that you will be translating the words of someone who ~~despises~~ who doesn't even like his language. No. Who doesn't even like his language is OK. Someone who doesn't even like his language and who has exiled himself ~~forever~~ since his teenage years. Sorry. That's too fatalistic. Who has exiled himself from his country to live in another. My Spanish is error-ridden, broken, wounded, full. Sorry. Please forgive me. How lucky I am to be able to correct myself. If you're going to plagiarise, better to show one's scars. A Spanish in which I am only able to understand myself when I write it but which I don't get on with at all orally. And so, from the off, I beg of you all to accept my thanks and apologies.

Out of nowhere, I was interrupted by a call.

It was Igor.

...

—

14.

In the original text, Marlowe is male.

—

15.

In the original text, the four singers Sergio mentions wanting to be are Roberto Carlos, Camilo Sesto, Perales and Dyango. I chose to stick with four male singers but make them singers a British audience would recognise. I also chose to stick with four crooners... and that at least one should feel cheesy.

—

20.

The original poem by Idea Vilariño is as follows in Spanish

Decir no

decir no

atarme al mástil

pero

deseando que el viento lo voltee

que la sirena suba y con los dientes

corte las cuerdas y me arrastre al fondo

diciendo no no no

pero siguiéndola.

—

21.

In the original text, Sergio thinks of Gabriel. Gabriel Calderón.

—

22.

Gabriel, Hi.

What's up?

I'm calling from Ljubljana.

From where?

From Ljubljana.

What's that?

It's a capital city. It's the capital of Slovenia.

I don't believe you.

It's true. And I'm calling you because I want to tell you something. A new idea. A new play. A new project that I would like for us to do together. And... That's all I wanted to say. When I get back to the hotel, I'll send you an email and I'll tell you more.

Great. Sounds good. I'm up for it, whatever it is. And I also have something to tell you. Something very important. Nobody knows. You'll be the first to know.

I'll guess. You're going to be a dad.

Yes. We're pregnant. But nobody knows. How did you know?

It doesn't matter. How are you feeling?

I... I don't know... sometimes.

Come on, don't be gay. I don't know if you're going to be a good dad but being a dad is going to make you a better writer.

Don't tell anyone.

No one. Cross my heart and hope to die.

You're an atheist.

I'm in the middle of a forest. If I speak a word, I'll hang myself from a tree.

Jesus Christ, Sergio!

The only thing is, for this play, you're going to have to shave your beard.

Is it another one of your auto-fictions?

I'll tell you later.

So I'm going to be you.

No. No. Not me. You'll be a character that is me. That's different.

First Saffores. Now me. Every time, it's someone younger and younger.

I hadn't thought about it that way. Maybe. I'm becoming another Dorian Gray.

I've never read it.

Haven't you. You should. In the prologues, there's one of the most beautiful things ever said about art. Something along the lines of all art is perfectly useless.

I don't think that.

I know. It's your only fault. I do. I'm sure that art is completely useless. Anyway, I'll write as soon as I get back to the hotel. A kiss.

Another.

—

23.

In the original script, the song Sergio sings to Gabriel is 'Corazón mágico' by Dyango. The lyrics may be found online.

—

26.

...

When the sushi arrived, I switched channels to the news and started to eat my sushi in front of Rafa Nadal winning his ninth French Open, the damaging of some Giotto frescoes by an Islamic State terrorist and the abdication of

King Juan Carlos of Spain. First a Pope had stepped aside.
Now a King. What strange times we lived in.

...

—

35.

*In my adaptation I cut the two middle paragraphs of this chapter.
In the original script, chapter 35 was as follows.*

Very well, he said, and after a brief look around to check
no one was listening, he began to tell his tale with that
coldness that comes naturally to those who work with the
dead.

Everything he told me that afternoon was awful to have
to listen to. To be sat there, in that café, listening to such a
story, was terrible for me. What he was telling me was truly
horrific.

Marlowe was right. It was much worse than could be
imagined. Everything that Marlowe had suggested had
happened had indeed happened. She had been absolutely
right about the victim's body having been cut up into bits
by a sharp knife. Just by looking at the stains, Marlowe
had been able to discover everything that the ex-head of
Slovenia's police force was now telling me.

I'm going to try to reproduce his account as accurately as
possible.

—

EPILOGUE

It was three in the afternoon on a Saturday in Montevideo when I answered my phone. It was Gonzalo Marulli.

Did you hear about what happened to Sergio?, he said.

I didn't know what to say. I said nothing. I could only listen in silence.

That night, I wanted to go to see his mother, but everyone said no. That it was better not to go. They'd tried to explain to her what had happened, but she hadn't understood what they were talking about.

It's better like this, said Sergio's sisters. It's better she doesn't understand.

All that night, I didn't know what to do. We all called each other. Minutti. Mariana. Grompone. Not one of us could believe that it was true. We all thought it was a lie. That it was just another one of Sergio's auto-fictions.

A few days later the Ministry of Culture asked me to go to Ljubljana in my capacity as director of the NIDA – you see I was the director of The National Institute of Dramatic Arts at the time – to go to Ljubljana to be present at Sergio's cremation and to bring back the ashes to Montevideo.

Two days later I was on a plane to Ljubljana, via Paris, landing some 16 hours later in a city I hadn't even known existed just a few days before.

As I came out of arrivals, there was a man from the embassy waiting for me with a car and he drove me to a hotel.

This hotel.

This room.

This very room here.

Then I did what I always do when I arrive at a hotel where I am going to be staying for a while. I unpacked my suitcase. I prepared my desk. I plugged in my computers, and I got the wifi connected on all my machines. I wanted to call home.

Everything was OK back home. On Skype, I could see her belly and that was the only thing I wanted to do. Look at her belly.

The next day, a Sunday, the same embassy man and the same embassy car came to pick me up and he drove me to the crematorium of Ljubljana's central cemetery. The incineration was to take place at ten that morning.

It was all very quick.

They made me go into a room where there was a closed coffin. The room was cold. I stood by the box and I couldn't take my eyes off it for a few minutes.

Eventually my gaze shifted and I noticed a Bible on a small table next to the coffin. It was the only possible source of comfort in the entire room. Even for me, who couldn't even believe that anyone could believe. I opened it and flicked through it. My hands falling upon the pages most worn. They must have been the pages most read in this place. It was the book of Ecclesiastes and there was a passage marked out in yellow highlighter. It said, 'For the living know they will die; but the dead know nothing, for in the grave, whither thou goest, there is no work, nor device, nor knowledge, nor wisdom'.

Then one of the crematorium employees came up to me and explained to me in a solemn voice that in two minutes he would be switching on the conveyer belt which would move the coffin into the incinerator.

So now I only had two minutes. I didn't know what to do. So I stretched out my hand and placed it on the coffin and I began to caress it as if I was caressing him. I don't like to be caressed, Sergio would always say to me. I don't like being touched. And now that's what I was doing. Now I was moving my hand up and down where I imagined his body to be.

And that was when I saw a metal plate that said:

Sergio Blanco

Montevideo 1971 - Ljubljana 2014

The crematorium assistant moved towards a metal platform where there was an electronic desk with a number of screens and buttons, and after a small nod of the head, he activated the system.

The coffin began to ever so slowly creep its way on the metal conveyor belt and as it approached the wall, with perfect timing, a small shiny metal door slid up to allow the box to enter the oven.

Everything went like clockwork.

Once the coffin was completely inside, the shiny metal door slid back down and the only thing you could hear was the deafening roar of the gas flames bursting into life, deadened by the thickness of the metal walls of the oven.

The assistant once again came up to me and explained that if I wished to see the incineration taking place inside the oven, there was a little window on the side, for precisely that purpose.

I thought about it for a moment but finally decided that Sergio probably wouldn't have wanted me to. Whenever we would go to the swimming pool, he would always turn away from me as he got undressed. He didn't like to be watched.

Less than half an hour later, the same assistant appeared with an urn and gave it to me. It was still warm. You could still feel the heat within.

After that he asked me to sign some papers, then shook my hand in a very friendly manner and told me I was free to go.

The chauffeur was waiting for me outside the cemetery. I got in the car, and holding the urn in my lap, I asked to be taken back to the hotel.

Once back in my room, I placed the urn on the desk and thought to myself that it was strange to be there with Sergio's ashes. We'd been in so many hotel rooms together. In Buenos Aires, in Chile, in Colombia, in Mexico, in Madrid, Athens. This would be the last time we shared a room.

Turning around I realised that on the bed lay Sergio's suitcase with all his belongings. I was going to have to take it back with me to Montevideo.

Of course, I opened it to look for what I then found. The text of this play. I knew that Sergio was obsessed with printing out copies of his plays as he wrote them. And there it was, printed out. The entire play.

I threw myself on the bed and began to read. I devoured the text in one go, bristling with envy at not having written the play myself. It was perfect, beautiful, brilliant, like everything that Sergio wrote.

When I finished it, I remained still for a moment. Nobody else apart from me knew that this text even existed.

I thought about claiming it for myself. I could easily change the name. Remove Sergio Blanco and sign it with Gabriel Calderón. I was tempted.

Then I thought about making it worse. That way, Sergio's last play would go down in history as a bad play. Sergio Blanco's worst play.

And then, I thought that actually the best thing to do was to leave it as it was but include a prologue and maybe a bit in the middle in which he would say that he'd written the play for me and that he wanted me to perform it.

So I sat down at the desk and I began to retouch it. I changed a few things, a few dates, little things here and there. In the end, I added quite a lot, I made sure my name Gabriel Calderón appeared quite a few times throughout, and when I was happy with all the little modifications I'd made, I put it back into the suitcase.

His final text was now a text that he'd written for me. I liked that. A lot. His last text would be dedicated to me.

...

—

APPENDIX III

Sergio's original foreword to the first edition in Spanish and English:

—

Durante el mes de mayo del 2014 me encontré dando una conferencia sobre el mito de Narciso en la Universidad de Liubliana en Eslovenia, dentro del marco de un encuentro internacional europeo en torno al tema de El mito y la mirada. Durante los días que duró el congreso, nació la idea de este texto a partir de una mancha de sangre que descubrí en la moquette de la habitación de mi hotel. El ultimo día que estuve en esa extraordinaria ciudad, escribí un correo a las dos personas que me habían acompañado en esa estadía eslovena, mis entrañables amigos españoles Sonsoles Herreros Laviña y José Luis García Barrientos, en el cual les contaba la idea de la pieza que se me acababa de ocurrir. Al mes siguiente en una estadía profesional de diez días en La Habana empecé y terminé la escritura de este texto. Cada mañana lo iba escribiendo en mi hotel y a la tarde le iba contando las escenas a mi amigo e inmenso dramaturgo cubano Abel González Melo, quien venía a buscarme para llevarme al seminario que estaba dictando en la Universidad de La Habana.

A ellos tres, que asistieron al origen de este texto, se lo dedico con toda mi admiración, mi amor y mi agradecimiento. A ellos tres, Sonsoles, José Luis y Abel, vayan estas palabras escritas desde el desasosiego y desgarro más profundos.

Y a Gabriel, por supuesto, a Gabriel Calderón, mi amigo, mi hermano, mi otro yo.

—

During the month of May 2014 I found myself giving a talk on the myth of Narcissus at the University of Ljubljana in Slovenia, as part of an international conference on Myth and the Gaze. The idea for this play came during my stay in Ljubljana when I discovered a blood stain on the carpet of my hotel room. On the last day of my stay, I wrote an email to my two dear Spanish friends Sonsoles Herreros Laviña and José Luis García Barrientos, who had been with me in Slovenia, explaining to them the idea I'd just had for a new play. The next month, I had a ten day writer's residency in Cuba. It was there that I started to write this play and where I finished it too. Every morning, I wrote it sitting at a desk in my hotel room, and in the afternoon I'd share what I'd written with my friend, the incredible Cuban playwright Abel González Melo, as we walked together to the University of Habana where I was giving a series of afternoon classes.

It is to these three dear friends, who were there at the birth and delivery of this play, that I dedicate this work with all my admiration, all my love and all my thanks. It is thanks to Sonsoles, José Luis and to Abel, that these words emerged from restless, shifting plates, deep deep down in the dark.

And to Gabriel, of course, to Gabriel Calderón, my friend, my brother, my other I.

APPENDIX IV

All my love and thanks to:

Cordelia Grierson, Russell Lucas, Trevor White, Alex Austin, Philippe Koscheleff, Roxi White

Thanks also to my family, to the entire creative team who worked on this show, to all the staff at the Pleasance, especially to Nic Connaughton.

And to Sergio, of course, to Sergio Blanco, my friend, my brother, my other I.

La Ira de Narciso was first performed was on 26th February 2015 at Auditorio Sodre, Montevideo, Uruguay, with the following cast and crew.

Written and directed by Sergio Blanco
Performed by Gabriel Calderón

Video design	Miguel Grompone
Set, costume and lighting	Laura Leifert and Sebastián Marrero
Vocal coaching	Sara Sabah
Sound production	Tato Martínez
Assistant director	Inés Cruces
Graphic design	Polder

Produced by Complot – Adrián Minutti & Matilde López

WWW.OBERONBOOKS.COM

Follow us on Twitter @oberonbooks
& Facebook @OberonBooksLondon